This Boxer Books paperback belongs to

. . . .

www.boxerbooks.com

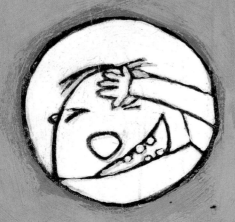

For John
Manuela Olten

This paperback edition published in 2008

First published in Great Britain in 2007
by Boxer Books Limited.
www.boxerbooks.com

First published as *Echte Kerle* by Bajazzo Verlag, Zurich 2004

Original text and illustrations copyright © 2004 Manuela Olten

Original translated text copyright © 2007 Boxer Books Limited

The right of Manuela Olten to be identified as the author
and illustrator of this work has been asserted by her
in accordance with the Copyright, Designs and Patents Act 1988.

ISBN 10: 1-905417-66-7
ISBN 13: 978-1-905417-66-7

1 3 5 7 9 10 8 6 4 2

Printed in China

BOYS
ARE BEST!

Manuela Olten

Boxer Books

They spend all day combing their **dolls' hair!**

And changing their dolls' clothes!

On and off

on

on

on

off

off

off

off off

on on

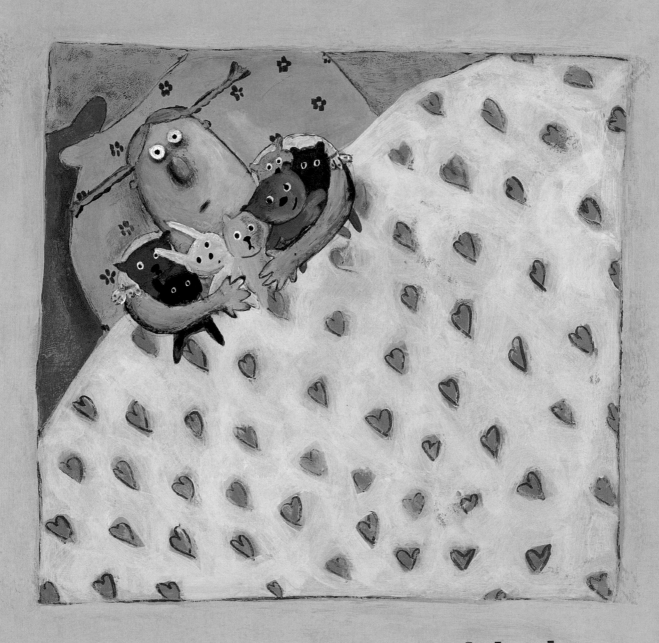

Girls take their silly teddy bears to bed with them every night.

Girls are such

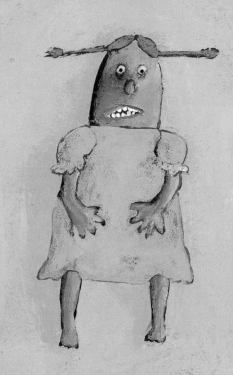

they wet their pants!

Girls are even scared of

ghosts!

Oh.

Um... I have to go to
the bathroom...

Boys are so silly!

Other Boxer Books paperbacks

Big Smelly Bear: **Britta Teckentrup**

Big Smelly Bear never washed, brushed or took a bath.
Big Smelly Bear was followed by a big smelly stink
wherever he went.
Until one day he met a new friend.
Could she persuade Big Smelly Bear to take a bath?
ISBN13: 978-1-905417-43-8

Duck & Goose: **Tad Hills**

Duck and Goose find an egg. "Who does it belong to?"
they ask. A delightfully funny tale, with rich paintings
and strong main characters.
Parents everywhere will recognise this tale of
one-upmanship, which firmly establishes the positive
aspects of learning to share.
ISBN13: 978-1-905417-26-1

Wait! I want to Tell a Story: **Tom Willans**

"Wait! I want to tell you a story!" said the muskrat.
"Okay," said the tiger, "but make it quick!"
Tom Willans' first picture book is indelibly
stamped with the hallmarks of a read-aloud classic.
ISBN10: 0-9547373-7-7